The chas

The Goog slowed down on the second floor stairs. After he hobbled to the bottom, he finally stopped.

"Easy," Harry whispered as we looked over the railing.

Harry and I crept down the last few steps. We were getting so close. Tiptoe... tiptoe...

Just as Harry reached out for his cat, The Goog leaped to the left, then ducked into the last room on the first-floor hall.

Harry and I stopped at the door.

We had *never* been inside *this* room before.

"We can't go in there, Harry!" I said. "Kids are not allowed. It's for teachers only!"

Harry looked me in the eye. "We have to. We have no choice. We have to rescue The Goog. Let's go, Doug!"

BOOKS ABOUT HORRIBLE HARRY

Horrible Harry and the Ant Invasion
Horrible Harry and the Christmas Surprise
Horrible Harry and the Dragon War
Horrible Harry and the Drop of Doom
Horrible Harry and the Dungeon
Horrible Harry and The Goog
Horrible Harry and the Green Slime
Horrible Harry and the Holidaze
Horrible Harry and the Kickball Wedding
Horrible Harry and the Mud Gremlins
Horrible Harry and the Purple People
Horrible Harry at Halloween
Horrible Harry Goes to Sea
Horrible Harry Goes to the Moon
Horrible Harry in Room 2B
Horrible Harry Moves Up to Third Grade
Horrible Harry's Secret

Horrible Harry and The Goog

BY SUZY KLINE

Pictures by Frank Remkiewicz

PUFFIN BOOKS

Special appreciation . . .

To the schools I visited in Clarkston, Michigan, for
inspiring many of the details in the teachers' lounge,
and Smithville Elementary School in Galloway, New
Jersey, for the special details of the boiler room.

PUFFIN BOOKS
Published by the Penguin Group,
Penguin Young Readers Group, 345 Hudson Street, New York, New York 10014, U.S.A.
Penguin Group (Canada), 90 Eglinton Avenue East, Suite 700, Toronto, Ontario, Canada M4P 2Y3
(a division of Pearson Penguin Canada Inc.)
Penguin Books Ltd, 80 Strand, London WC2R 0RL, England
Penguin Ireland, 25 St Stephen's Green, Dublin 2, Ireland (a division of Penguin Books Ltd)
Penguin Group (Australia), 250 Camberwell Road, Camberwell, Victoria 3124, Australia
(a division of Pearson Australia Group Pty Ltd)
Penguin Books India Pvt Ltd, 11 Community Centre, Panchsheel Park, New Delhi - 110 017, India
Penguin Group (NZ), Cnr Airborne and Rosedale Roads, Albany, Auckland 1310, New Zealand
(a division of Pearson New Zealand Ltd)
Penguin Books (South Africa) (Pty) Ltd, 24 Sturdee Avenue, Rosebank,
Johannesburg 2196, South Africa

Registered Offices: Penguin Books Ltd, 80 Strand, London WC2R 0RL, England

First published in the United States of America by Viking,
a division of Penguin Young Readers Group, 2005
Published by Puffin Books, a division of Penguin Young Readers Group, 2006

13 15 17 19 20 18 16 14

Text copyright © Suzy Kline, 2005
Illustrations copyright © Frank Remkiewicz, 2005
All rights reserved

LIBRARY OF CONGRESS CATALOGING-IN-PUBLICATION DATA IS AVAILABLE.

Puffin Books ISBN 0-14-240728-3

Printed in the United States of America

My Dear Reader,

This past year I got to visit schools in Alabama, Connecticut, Illinois, Kentucky, Maine, Massachusetts, Michigan, New Jersey, New Hampshire, and New York. At each one, I asked the students the same question: What place in your school would you _love_ to go to, but have never been? It didn't matter which school or state the students were from—they all had the same answers.

You'll find out which places those are because Harry and Doug end up in each one chasing Harry's cat.

Keep loving books!

♡ Love,
Suzy Kline

*Dedicated with love to my beautiful
daughter, Jennifer Kline DeAngelis.
You are the world to me!*
—Mom

Contents

The Goog

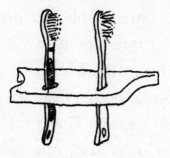

My name is Doug, and I'm in third grade. I write about what happens in Room 3B. Usually my stories are about my best friend Harry, who likes to do horrible things.

I never thought I'd write about Harry's cat.

He's the reason Harry and I had our first adventure after school.

He's the reason we ended up in places

at South School where we weren't supposed to be!

I can't wait to tell you all about it. But first, there are a few things you need to know about Harry's cat.

He likes to do horrible things too.

His real name is Googer. Harry calls him The Goog, and, once in a while, Googie.

I think he looks scary. He has clumps of gray hair that stick together. Harry says that happens when cats get old and can't groom themselves very well.

Harry thinks The Goog's hairdo is cool.

I feel sorry for The Goog.

Last summer, he lost one eye and hurt his leg when he got caught in a Dumpster. The lid came right down on him. He was lucky to escape alive!

I went with Harry to the animal hospital when The Goog was being operated on. I remember Harry made a "Get Well Googie" card in the waiting room. It had a lot of water spots on it because he was crying so much.

The vet stitched up The Goog's left eye, and he was fine afterwards. He just teetered when he walked or ran.

Harry and I tried walking around one day like The Goog. We wanted to know what it felt like. It was hard to see with one eye. We didn't like it, so we just limped.

Harry takes good care of his cat.

He even brushes The Goog's teeth.
Googer has his own toothbrush. It's
right next to Harry's in the bathroom.
But that's not the only thing that
grosses me out.

When The Goog is licking himself,
sometimes he swallows hair and then
coughs it up. I hate hairballs, but they
don't bother Harry. He wipes them up
off the rug, and looks at them closely.
"Way to go, Goog!" he cheers.

I have to say, though, I have learned a lot about cats from Harry. He knows The Goog has five toes on his front paws and four toes on his back paws. Harry told me cats can see six times better than people in the dark.

He also told me cats have nose-prints instead of fingerprints. Harry said that's important for detectives to know. Harry thinks he's a detective sometimes. He even carries a plastic magnifying glass and mini flashlight in his pocket.

Well, getting back to my story, I never thought The Goog would come to school. Usually he spends the day with Harry's grandmother. She bakes things in her kitchen and sells them. The Goog likes the smell of food, and the kitchen is a warm place for him during the winter. He also gets to lick the dirty dishes.

But today was different.

Harry's grandmother came to South School, and The Goog followed her.

What's Going On in the Library?

The first part of my story involves a mystery.

Our class was just coming back from lunch recess. Miss Mackle was leading us down the hall. Harry and Mary and I were at the end of the line.

"Look!" Mary whispered. "There's a sign on the library door. It says it's closed for the rest of the day."

"Did you see that?" I asked. "Mrs.

Michaelsen just pulled down the shade on her library door."

"Something's going on in the library," Mary concluded. "I wonder what."

"Something secret," Harry replied as we stepped into Room 3B.

We kept whispering while we hung up our winter coats, wool scarves, and caps on the coatrack. "I wonder *when*," Mary said.

"After school," Harry answered, flinging his cap high on the shelf.

"*After school?*" Mary and I repeated.

"Yup," Harry explained. "I've got the scoop."

Other kids gathered around Harry as he spoke in a low voice. "My grandmother is coming at three fifteen. She told me she was baking a special cake for South School. But she wouldn't tell me why. She also said Doug and I could play checkers in the hall while she served refreshments in the library."

"Oh, pooh!" Mary groaned. "I wish I could stay with you."

"Me too," Ida said.

"I saw Mr. Cardini sneak into the library earlier today with a rolled-up poster," Dexter added. "Do you think it's a picture of Elvis?"

"I doubt it, Dex," Ida replied.

"What's the date today?" Mary demanded.

"February first," Song Lee said. "It isn't a holiday."

Sid held up a finger. "I bet they're having a party for the teachers after school."

"Or," ZuZu added, "a party for *one* teacher."

Harry nodded. ZuZu was the sharp new student who moved to Room 3B in December. He and Harry liked to think hard.

"I bet I know!" Mary exclaimed.

"Some teacher is turning forty or fifty. Mr. Cardini's poster probably says, 'Over the hill.' That's what the sign said for my aunt Hilda when she turned forty."

"I like going over the hill," Song Lee said. "There's a beautiful view."

Before any of us could explain to Song Lee what that meant, Miss Mackle motioned for us to hurry up. "Time for math!" she called.

Harry shrugged. "Well," he whispered, "Doug and I will give you guys the details tomorrow."

Mary got a long face.

When the three-o'clock bell rang, the only ones smiling were Harry, me, and Miss Mackle. Nobody wanted to go home. Not the kids that ride the bus or the kids that walk.

Mary was the last one to say good-bye to us. "You'd better tell us every juicy detail tomorrow!"

Then she gritted her teeth and muttered, "Some people are sooooo lucky."

The Goog Comes
to School

I *was* feeling lucky. I go to Harry's house every Wednesday to play. But today we got to stay after school for a while.

The whole adventure got started when we were sitting on the back steps of South School, just waiting for Harry's grandmother.

Our custodian was bending over, putting a doorstop in the door.

"Hi, Mr. Beausoleil!" Harry said.

When he stood up, he greeted us. "Hi, boys! Hold your nose; I've got some smelly bags of garbage."

I held my nose.

Harry didn't, of course. He loves horrible smells. "Is that leftover fish sticks?"

"Yup. And leftover broccoli."

"Eeeyeew," I moaned.

Just as our custodian hauled the garbage out to the Dumpster, Harry's grandmother pulled up in her red pickup truck. She parked it in the teachers' parking lot and headed our way. She was wearing a winter sweater and an apron that said A-1 CAKES. I couldn't keep my eyes off the big white box in her arms. It was so huge!

"That rascal!" Harry exclaimed. "He's done it again!"

"What?" I said.

"I'll take care of it!" Harry snapped. Then he ran to his grandma and gave her a big hug.

"Hi Lamb Chop," she said. She flashed a toothy smile, just like Harry does. "Hi, Doug!"

"Hi, Grandma Spooger."

"Let's hurry on in, boys," she replied. "A-1 Cakes can't be late."

As soon as we got to the library, she told Harry to take out his checkers from his backpack. "Have fun in the hallway here, boys. I shouldn't be more than ten minutes cutting this cake."

"What's going on?" I blurted out. "Is someone turning forty?"

"I don't think so," Grandma Spooger replied. "This is no birthday party. Be good, boys."

As soon as she went inside the library, I looked at Harry. He had quickly lined up two rows of black checkers and two rows of red on the board.

"I thought you were a detective. How come you didn't ask your grandma any questions?"

Harry put his nose next to mine. "You're on the wrong case, Doug-o!" he groaned. "Let's go!"

I shrugged as I followed Harry down the hall to the back entrance of the school. Mr. Beausoleil had taken the doorstop away.

"My grandma didn't bring just a cake to school," Harry groaned. "She brought The Goog too, only she didn't know it."

"He was in the truck?"

"In the back," Harry said, opening the door. "He hopped a ride. He does it all the time!"

"Why didn't you tell your grandma?"

"She was too busy. I knew I could rescue The Goog on my own. I've done it before."

As I held the door, Harry stepped outside and looked in one direction only. "Yup," he whispered. "There he is."

I couldn't believe my eyes!

There was The Goog, sniffing around the Dumpster. The lid at the top was still open.

"He loves fish sticks," Harry grumbled. "Stay here and hold the door, Doug. I'll be right back!"

I watched Harry sneak down the school steps and then tiptoe over to his cat. The Goog was looking up at the top of the Dumpster and getting ready to leap. His tail was tucked under him.

Harry lunged forward and grabbed The Goog. "Aha! Gotcha, Googie!" he exclaimed, holding him tight.

Harry scolded his cat all the way back up the school steps. "You did it again! You jumped in the back of Grandma's truck. This time you got a free ride to South School. So you thought you'd get a few leftover fish sticks, huh?"

The Goog put his paws on Harry's shoulder. He seemed to be content for the moment.

Harry kept bawling him out. "Do you want to lose another eye? Huh?"

Just as Harry stepped inside the school, I let the door close. The slamming noise startled The Goog. He leaped out of Harry's arms and raced down the hall.

The chase was on!

The Goog Chase!

Harry and I took off!

Our legs motored down the hall.

The Goog limped as he ran ahead. His ears stuck out like jet wings. Seconds later all we saw was a gray blur!

When he got to the end of the first floor, The Goog skidded into a quick turn. His claws made a scratching noise on the shiny wood floors. *Screeeeeeetch!* Then he bolted up the stairs.

"Doesn't your cat know we're not supposed to run in the halls?" I asked.

"The Goog has his own rules," Harry replied. "Follow that tail!"

We raced up the stairs, huffing and puffing. We could barely keep up with that gray ball of fur.

When The Goog got to the second floor, he picked up more speed.

"Rev your engines, Doug!" Harry said

when we got to the top. "Pretend we're 747 jets taking off on a runway."

Boy did we fly!

As soon as The Goog got to the end of the hall, he skidded into another turn.

The Goog slowed down on the second-floor stairs. After he hobbled to the bottom, he finally stopped.

Harry and I put the brakes on as we went down after him.

"Easy," Harry whispered as we looked over the railing. The Goog was in the same spot. "Easy does it, Doug-o."

Harry and I crept down the last few steps. We were getting so close. Tiptoe . . . tiptoe . . .

Just as Harry reached out for his cat, The Goog leaped to the left, then ducked into the last room on the first-floor hall.

Harry and I stopped at the door.

It was ajar.

We had *never* been inside *this* room before.

"We can't go in there, Harry!" I said. "Kids are not allowed. It's for teachers only!"

Harry looked me in the eye. "We have to. We have no choice. We have to rescue The Goog. Let's go, Doug!"

Invading the Secret Room

Slowly, I followed Harry around the door into the secret room. It was the teachers' lounge!

Harry quickly closed the door behind us. He wanted to trap his cat. The Goog was clawing at the couch. We plopped down next to him. We were pooped!

"This teachers' lounge has just been painted. I can smell it." Harry said. "It's cool, huh?"

"It's off-limits!" I snapped. "We're not supposed to be in here. We're not teachers."

Harry put his feet up on the back of the couch. "We can lounge in the lounge for a little while. It's a detective's dream! Look around!"

"For two minutes," I bargained.

Harry held up two fingers and nodded. "Look up there on the blue wall, Doug. There's writing in those three white painted clouds. I can't read cursive very well. You read it."

I looked up and read the first quote. "It says, 'Life isn't a matter of milestones, but of moments.' What's a milestone, Harry?"

"Some kind of rock, I think. My grandma will know. What do the other two clouds say?" Harry asked.

"The puffy one says, 'A smile is a

curve that sets everything straight.' I like that one!"

Then I read the third quote. "The biggest cloud says, 'To the world you might be one person, but to one person you might be the world.'"

Harry beamed. "Grandma says I'm her world." Then he added, "And her pork chop."

"I thought it was lamb chop."

"Same thing. A chop's a chop."

We got up and walked over to the two long tables that had plastic tablecloths. On top were three leftover cupcakes. The Goog was already on the table, sniffing them. He didn't seem tired at all. He still hadn't rested.

Harry took out his magnifying glass and looked closely at something on the tablecloth.

"Salt and pepper?" I asked.

"Sprinkles," Harry observed. "Probably fell off those birthday cupcakes."

I couldn't resist. I poked one. "Man, these cupcakes are hard!"

The Goog wasn't interested in the leftovers either. He jumped off the table, then rubbed up against the snack machine.

Harry and I followed the cat and looked behind the glass door. There were lots of little compartments. Each one had a snack sitting in it. "Wow! These cost fifty cents," Harry said. "Just look at all the different bags of stuff."

I named each item. "Barbecue potato chips, oatmeal cream cookie, potato skins with bacon and cheddar, popcorn, nachos, bite-size fat-free pretzels, and *candy*!"

"Whoa," Harry replied. "That's some selection!"

"Those snacks aren't in that food pyramid we study for health. You know the fruit and vegetable group, the dairy group, the meat and poultry group, and the whole grains group," I said.

"That's a no-brainer," Harry answered. "Of course they are. Remember in math we learned that the pointy top of the triangle is called the apex? Well, that's where the snack group is. Right there at the top of the health pyramid." He was rubbing his hands together. I knew what he was thinking. He wished he had fifty cents. *Oh, Harry!* I thought.

The Goog walked over to the far

corner of the room where there was another door left ajar.

Harry and I watched the cat go inside.

"There must be another little room inside this teachers' lounge," I said.

When the cat didn't come out, Harry motioned to me. "Time to investigate, Doug."

"Wait a minute," I said. "It says REST-ROOM on the door. That's the teachers' bathroom! We can't go in there!"

Harry didn't hesitate.

He went inside.

It was deadly, but I did it! I followed Harry.

There was The Goog on top of the toilet tank, pawing at some flowers in a pot.

"They're fake," Harry said.

"If they're fake," I said, "how come

it smells like flowers in here?"

Harry picked up an aerosol can and sprayed it. "This is what the teachers use after . . ."

"Don't say it!" I interrupted.

"Okay, but my grandma just opens our bathroom window. We don't use this spray stuff," Harry added, setting the can back down.

Then Harry noticed a little round table with a book on it. "Gee," he said. "Teachers even read in the bathroom!"

"That's a weird title," I said. *"Polish Your Furniture with Pantyhose?"*

"My grandma would like that book," Harry said. Then he looked up. "Hey, no wonder the teachers use a spray. They have a fake window!"

I looked up at the bathroom wall. There was a big picture window painted on it with a view of boats in the water.

"How cool is that? It's a scene from Venice, Italy!" I said. "Those are gondolas. I remember reading about them in a book about canals."

Harry slapped me five. "Way to go, Doug!"

"Yeah, and now it's time for us to go, Harry. Two minutes is up."

We looked at The Goog. He was playing with the toilet paper roll. Harry picked him up gently and returned to the lounge.

On our way out, I noticed there were a lot of sign-up sheets on the bulletin boards. Harry pointed to one with big

letters—TGIF—that had the longest list of names. Even Miss Mackle's!

"What does TGIF stand for?" I asked.

Harry smiled. "The Goog is found."

"Right," I agreed.

As we headed down the hallway, I felt a tickle in my nose. It had to be from that bathroom spray. I tried to cover my mouth with my hand.

"Ah-chooo!"

My sneeze scared The Goog!

He jumped out of Harry's arms and scooted down the stairs to the basement.

Harry and I had to chase him again.

But this time, things looked spooky. The basement was dark, and we couldn't see as well as The Goog.

Ghosts in the Basement!

"This is creepy," I whispered. "I don't like going into the basement. We don't know where the light switch is down there."

Harry stopped in the middle of the stairway. "Doug," he said, "Miss Mackle brings us down here *every day*. It's where the bathrooms are. Every class on the first floor comes down here. It's like a school highway."

"I know that," I said, "but the lights are always on. It's dark down there now."

"Look," Harry said, taking something out of his back pocket. "I've got my trusty flashlight with me. We'll be just fine. We have to get The Goog!"

"Okay," I said, holding tight to the railing. I was glad Harry had his mini flashlight with him.

"What's that?" I said spotting something on the bottom step. "Is that a cockroach?"

Harry investigated with his flashlight.

"It's a penny, Doug."

"Oh."

"I'll flip it," Harry said, putting his flashlight under his armpit. "Heads or tails?"

"Tails," I called.

Harry tossed and caught the penny with one hand, then slapped it on his other. "Tails. It's yours!" he said, handing the penny to me.

I tucked it inside my pants pocket and crossed both fingers. *Be my lucky penny!* I wished.

As soon as we got to the basement, I stepped into the room that had a sink and soap. My hands were slimy from my sneeze.

"What are you doing, Doug?" Harry snapped.

"Washing my hands. Why?"

"You're doing it in the *girls' bathroom!*"

"*Aaaaaaaaaaaaauuuuuuuuugh!*" I

groaned, leaping out of there. I didn't care if I had wet hands.

"The boys' bathroom is on the other side, remember?"

"Yeah, yeah," I said, shaking my wet hands in the air. Then I reached into my pocket and pulled out the penny. "Here. You can have it, Harry."

It was not my lucky penny.

"Thanks, man!" Harry beamed.

He got right back to business.

"I bet The Goog went into the boiler room," Harry said. "See the door in the far corner? It was left half open."

"B-b-boiler room?" I replied. No one ever went inside there.

Except the custodian.

It was like his kingdom.

"The boiler room is warm," Harry said. "It's like Grandma's kitchen. Come on, Doug. We have to check it out."

I didn't like walking over there. It was a forbidden place!

Harry tapped the boiler room door wide open with his sneaker. At least it didn't squeak.

It had to be the darkest room in the school. There were no windows, and it was very warm.

As we tiptoed inside, I saw something moving around up high. "Wh-what's that?"

Harry spotlighted them with his flashlight.

"Flying white things," Harry observed.

"Ghosts!" I gasped. *"There are ghosts in the boiler room!"*

"Hold on, Doug. We have to let them know we're friends. I'll call their names."

"Gh-ghosts have names?" I asked, shivering behind Harry.

"Sure," he replied. "Haven't you heard of Casper the Ghost? He's friendly. I watch him on video. We might have a famous ghost in our boiler room."

I closed my eyes as I listened to Harry call out names.

"Casper?" he said.

There was no answer.

Harry tried other names. "Phil? George? Lulu?"

I inched closer to Harry. I was trembling.

"Oh, man!" Harry said.

"Wh-what?" I answered, opening my eyes slowly.

"Take a look, Doug-o. Up high."

Harry shined his flashlight on the ceiling.

"Rags!" I shouted. "Big white rags!"

"Yup. About a dozen of them. There's a washing machine over there, but no dryer. Mr. Beausoleil probably hangs the white rags on the pipes. It's warm enough down here to dry them."

Just as I took a deep breath and sighed, we heard footsteps. Someone was coming!

Suddenly the lights went on in the boiler room. "What are you boys doing down here?"

We both turned around. "Mr. Beausoleil!"

I was so glad to see him. "I'm sorry, Mr. Beausoleil," I said. "We should have asked permission to come into your boiler room."

"My cat is hiding somewhere," Harry explained. "We came down here to find him."

Mr. Beausoleil wasn't smiling. "You *never* go into the boiler room without an adult. Don't you know that?"

"Yes, sir," I answered. "I'm really sorry."

"I know that now, Mr. Beausoleil," Harry said. "I'm sorry too."

"Well, if you boys promise never to do it again, I'll try to help you."

"I promise," I said.

"I promise too. Cross my heart and hope to die. Stick a needle in my eye," Harry added.

We watched Mr. Beausoleil walk over to his corner office where he had a fan and a little refrigerator. He took out a small container of milk and poured it into a saucer.

Seconds later, The Goog came out from under one of the two big blue boilers and started lapping up the

milk. "I thought he was thirsty. It gets very warm down here. What's your cat's name?"

Harry smiled. "Googer."

After the cat drank the milk for one full minute, Mr. Beausoleil gently picked him up and carried him over to his desk. We watched him slide something out with his foot.

"I'm glad I keep this critter cage down here. It's a big help."

We watched him gently put The Goog inside and then latch the door. "You'd be surprised how many critters come into our school. Caught a squirrel once and a bat in the attic. This is about the third cat that has wandered down here."

"Well, he's safe now," Harry said. "Thanks, Mr. Beausoleil."

I noticed the bulletin board over his desk. "Are those pictures of your family?" I asked.

Mr. Beausoleil smiled for the first time. "My grandchildren. I have four! They're a few years younger than you."

"Neato," Harry said. Then he noticed some drawings that were pinned on the corkboard. "Hey, I drew that picture for you last year when I was in second grade."

"You sure did, Harry!" Mr. Beausoleil replied. "I liked what you wrote too."

I read the note below Harry's picture:

Mr. Bowsalay,
    Thanks for the five pensil stubs. I'm colekting them.
    You are the best castodean in the word.

Love, Harry

Harry beamed.

"Didn't that used to be in the library?" I asked as we walked by a big piece of furniture.

"It sure was. It's your old card catalog.

The library doesn't use it anymore, so I brought it down here. Open one of the long drawers."

"Is it okay, Mr. Beausoleil?" I wanted to double-check.

"Go ahead."

Harry pulled out one long drawer. "Wow! Look at all the nails!"

I pulled out the long drawer next to it. "Cool! Screws!"

The other drawers had a huge selection of washers, bolts, and nuts.

"I want to be a detective *and* a custodian when I grow up," Harry said. Then he flashed his white teeth.

Now, Mr. Beausoleil beamed.

As soon as we got upstairs, we spotted Grandma Spooger. She was looking for us.

The Whole Story
Doesn't End

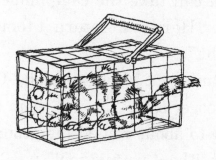

"Landsakes! Where have you boys been? You gave me the scare of my life!"

"Sorry, Grandma," Harry said, hugging her hard. "We were chasing The Goog."

"The Goog? He hopped another ride?" Grandma Spooger looked at Mr. Beausoleil's critter cage. She recognized the meowing.

"Googie, you are a rascal!" Then she put her finger through one of the holes and said, "My sweet little thing."

"You can take the cage home, Mrs. Spooger. Harry can return it tomorrow. It's light."

"Thank you, Mr. Beausoleil," Grandma Spooger said. "I'll give them a good talking-to about wandering around the school without permission!"

"They learned their lesson," he said. "They're good boys."

After we waved good-bye to Mr. Beausoleil, Grandma Spooger hugged us again. "So you must have had some tour of the building chasing that cat!"

"We sure did!" Harry answered. "It was one cool adventure! What's a milestone?"

"Where did you see that word?"

Harry told part of the truth. "We saw it written on a school wall."

"Really?" Grandma Spooger said. "Well, I wasn't going to say anything, but it's too perfect an example. The school staff was celebrating something very special in the library after school today.

"The *library*!" Harry and I exclaimed. We had almost forgotten!

"What was going on?" Harry blurted out.

"Well, a milestone is a very important event in someone's life. Today the staff was celebrating a milestone in your teacher's life."

"Yeah?" we eagerly replied.

"Miss Mackle is engaged to be married!"

"*Engaged?*" we said. "Whoa!"

"Who's the lucky guy?" Harry asked.

"I'll let her tell you in her own way," Grandma Spooger said with a twinkle in her eye, "in her own time."

"Pleeeeeeeeease tell us," Harry begged. He was down on his knees.

"It's time to go," Grandma Spooger insisted.

As we were about to walk by the library, we knew we had one last chance to take a very quick look. The door was wide open. Just maybe, we could see who the lucky guy was.

I saw the big poster that said CON-GRATULATIONS!

We saw Miss Mackle smiling and talking to three other teachers. All three were men!

"Which one, Doug?" Harry asked as we passed by the library door. "Which one is she engaged to? Is it Mr. Marks? He took her to that *Oklahoma* play."

"I don't know," I said. "She was standing next to Mr. Moulder, the sec-ond-grade teacher; Mr. Skooghammer,

the computer teacher; and Mr. Marks."

"Oh, man!" Harry groaned as we stepped outside the back door of the school.

And then he muttered the third quote in the teachers' lounge. "One of those guys thinks Miss Mackle is the world. Which one?"

The Goog meowed. He wanted to know too!

"You boys will find out soon enough," Grandma Spooger said with a chuckle. "I've told you too much already. Your teacher will decide when to share all the details of her happy news."

Harry and I dragged our feet to the truck.

"Well," I said. "Mary will be happy. She'll find out the juicy details tomorrow when we do."

Harry had a long face. I could tell he

wanted to be the first to know.

The Goog was making a throaty sound. He wasn't happy either!

But my story does have a sweet ending. Grandma Spooger saved us each a piece of Miss Mackle's engagement cake. We got to eat it in the truck, and The Goog got a lick of frosting.

It made us all smile.

And that curve kind of set everything straight.